Miniyarns

A Knot of Nano Stories

Athila Nabin

ISBN 979-8-89002-997-3

Dedication

To the one reading this…

Your smile is awesome; make it contagious too!

Acknowledgements

Publishing a book has been my dream for years! But as I write this, I have realized it is nothing short of a motherhood journey with lots of challenges and hardships yet feeling abundantly joyful when the book comes out from you! As Paul Coelho says in *The Alchemist*, "When you want something, the whole universe conspires in order for you to achieve it." I feel the Universe has finally conspired for me on its own timeline. Well, for some, the Universe is God, and for some, it is the people. For me, it is both. And it is time for me to be grateful.

My first thanks to you for choosing my book among the hundreds of books being published every day, and I sincerely hope you like it. The next in line would be none other than my husband Khaja for his love, kindness and patience — more than I deserve. He is my first audience and best critic. Sometimes, my co-author too! I would like to then thank the two superwomen in my life — my mother Sulaiha and my mother-in-law Rahila who didn't confine me to the kitchen and household chores but gave me wings to fly to my dreamland. My heartfelt gratitude to my father Abdul Karim and father-in-law Sheik Mohideen for their moral support. Thanks to my sister Sabeela, sister-in-law Parveen and their families for always being there for me. Of course, my little munchkins Rida and Raaid, my inspiration behind many stories, to whom I have more stories in store!

When no one recognized me, there was one who believed in me, showered encouraging words and sponsored the creation of my own website to post my writings, without whom I wouldn't have reached this far in life. My beloved uncle Mohamed Rafi, Founder and CEO of Princeton Vitamins LLC and Professors121, is also a founder of me, I would lovingly say. Thanks, Mama, and I am eternally indebted to you. I am obliged to thank my MP Family and the extended families for always being of immense support and giving me strength.

We may be a stone desperately wishing to be shaped but are afraid of the chisel strikes and hammer blows. But I chose the painless procedure to carve myself into communication and leadership skills — Toastmasters. Had it not been for the nano story contest by Toastmasters, where I first wrote some stories, the author in me wouldn't have poked out. And Toastmasters is not just that, but more like a family than friends. And the lessons from this forum of like-minded folks are my secret to rejuvenation and realizations in life.

Life is so strange that sometimes strangers become your life guides in a short time. And that stranger in my life who motivated and persuaded me to collate these works is Vikas Sinha, who has authored the bestsellers *The Case of the Missing Brother* and *The Case of the Stolen Tiara*. Thank you, Vikas Ji, for your honest opinions and guidance.

My heartfelt thanks to Sesu Dasse, Founder and CEO of Inspire Career Development Center, Pondicherry, with whom I am proud to celebrate over a decade of friendship. You had always insisted that I shelve out of my comfort zone and focus on my skills to achieve greater things in life. I believe this venture is probably my baby-steps of your vision.

I owe a lot to my friends for life from school and college, colleagues who braced me up beyond professional space and endearing sisters from my apartment for all their constant compliments and kind words that always encouraged me to write more. As much as I wish to name them all, it is impossible — not because I will miss out on anyone but just because the pages won't be sufficient!

The last person I wouldn't wish to miss is Gogul from ifuel technologies, who designed my website so elegantly, giving soul to my writings that garnered viewers from across the globe.

Little God

The little boy happily visited the temple with his grandmother, got coins from her and excitedly dropped them into the plates of the beggars seated outside the temple, and they blessed him in return. While praying inside, his grandmother advised him, "Ask God for more money so that you can give beggars more." And the little boy prayed aloud, "Dear God, make them all rich so that they don't beg!"

Love Knows No Race!

As the new neighbors moved in, her sweet voice tickled his ears, and her scent filled his breath. He jumped to see her, but the tall wall in between stood the villain. He climbed up the stairs for a glimpse of her face, and when she looked back, they knew what is love at first sight. Though they belonged to different races, they often escaped their homes and roamed around. On one such date, the brown skinned resting his head on the silky white her exclaimed, "Good that we're not humans, else we would have been chained for loving interracially!" the dog.

Father's Day

Some eyebrows raised questions. Some eyes expressed surprise. A few lips smirked, and others were pressed, puzzled. Not minding, she stood in the line with all the men ready for the race, with her son. She, the single mother, didn't want her son to miss his dad on Father's Day celebration. No matter who finishes first, she has already won!

His Plans

"Even God doesn't want me," he complained after a failed suicide attempt. God had rejected him for the second time, first being the horrible accident that killed his family, with him narrowly escaping. As he walked along the road weeping, he saw three puppies loitering around their dead mother, who was just run over by some vehicle. Empathizing the pain of being orphaned, he carried them home to make them his family. God smiled from above!

The Thrill

She was freshening up in the bathroom; he was eagerly waiting outside. The shower stopped, followed by the rhythmic trickle of water; he was thrilled at the thought of what was going to happen next. When she came out, he pushed her onto the bed, pounced on her and slit her throat, the psycho!

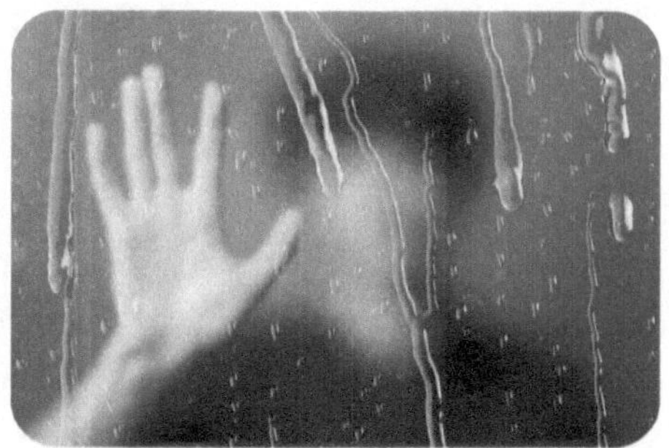

Karma

After twenty-five years, she regretted the words spoken. Her eyes welled up when she thought that her mother must have felt the same pain. Back then, when her mother had requested to teach her to read and write, being the first graduate of the family, she mocked, "What are you going to do learning that at this age?" Today, she heard the same words from her daughter when she asked her to teach how to use a smartphone.

Trans

"Mom, look at that uncle dressed up as an aunty," giggled the little boy at a transsexual person. He laughed aloud when ze was clapping and asking for money from the commuters. His mom advised him, "If you tease, ze'll continue to act funnily only. Try showing some love." The little boy smiled and waved his hands at Trans. Ze came, kept zir hands on his head and blessed him.

Blind Flute Seller

The blind man standing on the pavement under the scorching sun was playing the flutes and selling them for Rs. 20 each. With only ten flutes left, he rested under a shade and played a melancholy tune as mournful as his life. Just then, a passerby thrust a fifty-rupee note in the flute seller's hands even before he could protest and walked away. The blind flute seller, being the man of morals, then started selling the rest of his flutes for Rs. 15 each.

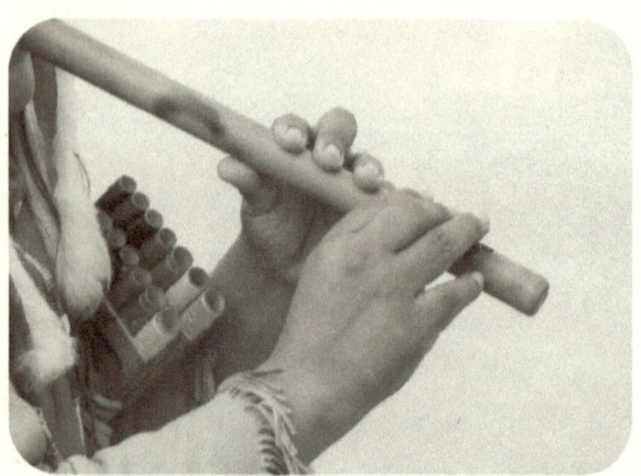

Forgive Me, My Ex!

She uncertainly answered the call from an unknown number and heard a distressed "Hello." Even after twenty-five years, she recognized the voice of the man she once dearly loved. With thousands of memories haunting her again and pain searing through her heart, she remained silent. "I'm sorry," he sobbed, "Sorry that I dumped you. I now feel your pain. My daughter attempted suicide and is battling for life as her boyfriend left her. Please forgive me. I want my daughter alive," he cried inconsolably. With tears flowing down, she replied in a trembling tone, "Bless her!" disconnected the call and let out an anguish wail.

Haunted By

Despite everyone's warning, he moved into the haunted house. That night, he heard strange sounds and creepy voices. Unusual smells suddenly filled the room. His things moved on their own. He saw shadows appearing out of the corner of his eyes. Though scared, he sighed, "At last, I'm not lonely anymore!" the forlorn young man.

The Special

"Our child is going to be special," said the childless couple to their parents on their way to the orphanage. The couple showed their parents a girl with leg braces whom they had decided to adopt, and their parents were horrified at the idea. Signing the adoption papers, the

father now prided, "Didn't we say ours is a '*Special child*'?"

The Accident

He was walking home fast, gratified by his collections for the day, which would feed his family for the next few days. Walking on the edge of the road, he didn't see the vehicle coming from behind and the last thing he heard was his own cry before being crushed. With his collected food scattered around, laid dead, the Ant!

Loves Me, Loves Me Not!

She saw her love interest at a distance and blushed. To find out if he loved her back, she started plucking the petals of the flower one by one, saying, "He loves me, he loves me not." and the last petal was "He loves me not.". "This is because it is even number

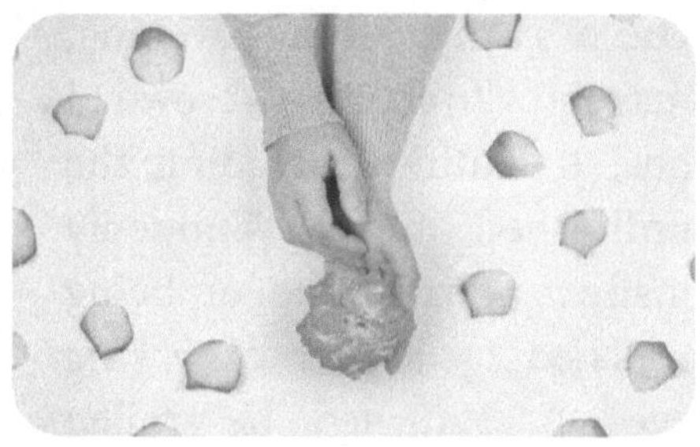

petalled," she tried convincing her disturbed heart. As she turned, he stood surprisingly smiling and extended a red rose, saying, "This has odd number of petals!"

Say Cheese!

Once again, the guests have visited the Home, this time to celebrate their son's birthday. The Father welcomed them, and the children adored the birthday boy's new dress. He cut the cake while the children sang the birthday song dissonantly. His parents then placed two bags of used clothes and old toys in front of them and exclaimed, "Say cheese!" with the camera flashing. The orphanage children shyly smiled, some hiding their patched clothing, some holding their buttonless shirts together and others staring at the cake!

The Book Love

On a rushy Friday evening, managing to stand in a crowded bus, I continued reading the unfinished novel. Suddenly instinct warned me of being watched by a pair of prying eyes. As I turned, he smiled and waved, holding the same novel - the love only felt by the book lovers.

Dignity

The poor vendor on the pavement was shouting at the top of his voice, trying to sell his vegetables, but passers-by bypassed him and walked

into the supermarket nearby. His throat dried up, and he picked up his water bottle. But seeing less water, he splashed them on the vegetables so they wouldn't be wrinkled like him. But his heart ached more than his throat, only to see people giving money to the beggar sitting idle next to him, not wanting to work and earn. Yet, the vendor continued his street cries until sunset, and then he packed all the limp vegetables and the dignity left!

Befriend

"I have a gift for you," said the young man, trying to befriend the little girl. Shoving it away, she ran into her room and slept whimpering. After some time, he quietly sneaked inside, went near her, kissed her cheeks, pulled the blanket over her, placed the gift near her and whispered, "Happy Birthday dear," the stepfather.

The Lust

When the lust was quenched, he started feeling guilty. "What did I just do?" he asked himself, sweaty. "I should have stayed within limits, but I was tempted. Whatever … I shouldn't have touched. I shall never do this again in my life." Swearing so, he, a highly diabetic man, thrashed the sweet box that he had just emptied eating into the dustbin.

Silent Suffering

She missed his loving looks and drooling cooks. She wished for his warm smiles and their walk together for miles. She longed for his care and caress, those passionate nights and silly fights. She wept inconsolably, who was neither a widow nor a divorcee but a poor wife who  just lost her husband's interest to another woman!

The Ladder

After a great struggle, he reached the hilltop. Exploring around, he finally found a broken ladder to climb up the rock on the hilltop where God is said to appear. As he reached, God miraculously appeared and asked how he got there. He replied proudly, "Because of my perseverance, grit and determination." God pushed him down to remind him of the ladder!

Strong Woman

When the young girl tripped into a pitfall, she wished someone would give her a helping hand. She longed for a consoling word and yearned to hear, 'Are you alright?' and panted for a gentle pat on her shoulders to move on. But when no one came to her rescue or solace, she struggled and got up by herself, bruised. Yet, she brushed off her shoulders, reassured herself that she was okay and strode her path. Then, a strong woman was born. No, made!

The Bedroom Moon

When I turned off my bedroom lights, the moon on the bed began to glow. My wife's face was like the moon: a perfect round, with dents and dark spots like the moon's surface, yet the most charming in the universe, but the light reflecting from her face was disrupting my sleep. Like the moon's gravitational pull causing tides, my emotions tided up, and I turned to her side. My hand slowly reached for hers and turned off her mobile.

Worth of Love

The little girl fearfully informed her parents that she had lost her new gold earring while playing in the park. Enraged that their hard-earned money was lost because of her carelessness, her parents chided and lashed her. Later, the lost earring was found after searching. But the little girl's love was lost forever!

His Workday

He woke up squinting his eyes to the sun's golden rays. He sipped his coffee, listening to the birds chirp. Praying his day to be good, he quickly showered, wore his pressed shirt and stepped out. By then, darkness had crept in, and the birds had rested in their nests. With his half of the world returning home, he started off to his night shift.

High Tech Kids

The horny wife, wanting to lure her husband, called their four-year-old son and asked, "Sweety, you want a baby brother or a baby sister?" The little boy replied excitedly, "Both." She smiled and whispered, "Go ask your daddy." He ran to his dad  and said, "I want a baby sister and a baby brother. Order them on Amazon!" As they lay down stupefied, he started sleeping in between them.

Painful Death

The searing pain radiating from her heart seeped throughout her body. She knew she was dying every minute but desperately wanted to live for her daughters. Unable to contain her emotion, she again wailed over her dead son, who committed suicide two months back. Dying once, he kept killing his loving mother for the rest of her life! 

Love Race

The bike racer rode his bike slowly with his lover as a pillion. The cool breeze ruffled his hair and fluttered her shawl. She poked his shoulders and chuckled, "Hey racer, drive fast and race up the time." He slightly turned his head toward her and replied

earnestly, "I wish the universe would slow down when you're with me!"

Venge

They were going to kill her. Soon, she'd also lay dead like her family, who were mutilated in front of her eyes. She couldn't move; she couldn't scream. The pain was excruciating with the continuous blows. Even then, she stood strong and smirked. "You'll all feel the heat soon," said the tree!

Grandmaaa...

An old lady from Chennai joined a spoken English course, and the class burst into laughter. Undeterred, she reasoned, "My son family in America come next month. Granddaughter not know Tamil." The next morning, son called and informed her that their vacation plan had been canceled. Though disheartened, she thought, "I'll learn and speak good English to my granddaughter when they come next year," and continued with her classes.

Double Standard

The actress danced sensually on-screen, uncovering her ivory skin. Stirred watching the movie, the man went to a whorehouse to gratify his desires. Society praised the actress for her performance, and she earned enough money to last another generation. The same society shamed the prostitute who just earned her next meal!

The Beautiful Couple!

The middle-aged wife was sadly looking at her increasingly graying hair in the mirror. Her husband, reading her thoughts, hugged her from behind, placed his chin on her shoulders and their cheeks brushed. "They're grays of wisdom!" he consoled.  She looked at her husband, who was going bald, and chuckled. Gently bumping her temple on his, she asked, "What about yours?" "Well, I'm growing young," he paused, and her eyebrows raised. He giggled and continued, "Into a baby!". They both laughed heartily, and the mirror saw the most beautiful couple!

One Last Time

She wished to hear from them; the phone never rang. She longed for their visit; they never turned up. She yearned for their time; they were too busy. She craved their care; they didn't mind. Today, her soul left for its heavenly abode, and when her body was about to be lifted to  the graveyard, they, her children, cried aloud, "One last time!"

Give Me a ...

"My sweetie, my cutie, give uncle a kiss," he cajoled his niece, showing his cheek. The toddler lisped, "No," shaking her head from side to side. He scooped her up, carried her to the nearby petty shop, bought her a lollipop and asked, "Now?" Excited, she planted a quick kiss, grabbed the lollipop and started enjoying the taste of candy and bribery!

Parentage

The father was worried that his daughter was working too hard, ignoring her health and not taking vacations. He wondered why she even had to toil when the money he had saved for her would last for generations to come. When he confronted his daughter, she replied, "Papa, your whole life, that's the way you showed me how to live."

The Secret Stalker

The little girl was shocked to see that man in their bedroom and her mom talking. She had seen him follow them whenever she and her mom went out alone. Perplexed, she inched near her mom and then saw

her talking to a photograph of the same man. The mom, seeing her daughter's quizzical look, explained that it was her late brother's picture and tearfully recalled their childhood memories. Smiling at his niece, the uncle's soul sitting nearby slowly faded away!

Perfect Targets

He secretly followed the strangers to the park and marked his aim at them. The woman as he studied was a nerdy, bubbly girl whose solitude was already killing her. The man, on the other hand, was thinking of taking his life after his recent breakup. *"Perfect targets!"* thought he, and shot the arrows of love, the Cupid!

Peace

Since the war began, all that the ten-year-old hiding in the basement heard was the sounds of air raid sirens, explosions, gunshots and warplanes streaking overhead. Suddenly, his shelter was bombed, and as the wall collapsed on him, he passed out. When he regained his

senses, he felt ultimate peace. There were no more bombings, no wails of injured and no cries of bereaved. But he was unable to move with an excruciating pain in his legs. When he finally managed to lift his torso from the rubble, he saw his neighborhood being shelled. Just then, he realized that he had not only lost his legs but also his hearing!

Guardian Angel

"You limped in the running race, brayed in the singing contest and scribbled in the drawing competition. What this time?" he heard his classmates mock as he climbed onto the stage. For this elocution competition, he had practiced and rehearsed well with his mother. But seeing the crowd, he froze like a statue, and his brain blanked out. Ignoring the ridiculing mutters, his mother reached him, patted his

back and said, "Don't worry if you can't speak in front of a crowd. You're definitely talented in one way or another way. Let's explore that. Cheers!"

Ravage

She lazily woke up late in the morning while the seagull was already actively looking for food. Collecting the milk packet, she snipped off the tip and prepared coffee. After disposing of the garbage, she sipped the warm coffee; it went down her throat, soothing her. The poor bird pecked the small clipped-off piece of milk cover, which got stuck in its throat, choking it!

Repentance

"Quit your job, and take care of kids. That is what you are for!" he recollected yelling at his wife last year. Repenting, he called her close, held her hands and whispered, "Sorry, you had a dream too. Go, earn your living. Stand on your own, and bring up our children well," wincing in pain from his advanced cancer.

Beauty

To welcome her marriage prospect and his family, she adorned the house with beautiful decorations that she made herself. She shined and rearranged her trophies and medals for them to admire. The aroma of the coffee and snacks she prepared invited their drool

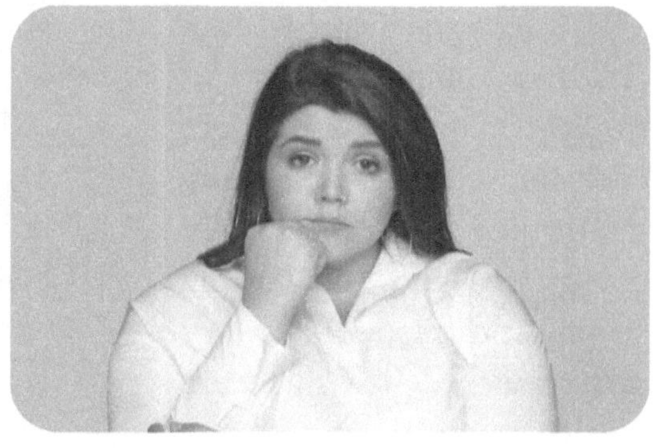

as they alighted the car. But all that they saw was her plump physique, and rejected her!

Being Single

"*Why hasn't Cupid struck me alone while my friends are dating even since high school?*" he wondered, sadly looking at the loving couples around him. Meanwhile, somewhere on the earth, his future wife prayed, "Dear God, let me be my husband's first crush and last love!"

The Longing

She longingly watched the children play happily in the park — swinging high, cheering to the sky, climbing up, thrilled to slide, excitedly going up and down the seesaw and filled with merry and no worry. "I wish I were like these kids!" sighed the girl in the wheelchair.

Soul of Love

He followed his wife secretly and saw her meet their family friend, whom he knew to be a perfect gentleman. To his surprise, the friend proposed to his wife suddenly but modestly. Though it was not as romantic as how he had proposed to his wife before their marriage, he saw her blush the same way. Seeing his wife fall in love again and the friend promising to take care of his widowed wife and their son, the husband's soul left the earth happily!

Genes

The child's eyes welled up and were ready to burst into tears anytime. With the stick in his father's hand swaying back and forth, his throat went dry, and he sucked his lips. "What's India's national animal?" asked the enraged father. "Lion," replied the boy in a feeble voice. As the father got infuriated at son's incorrect answer yet again, even  after teaching him a hundred times, the grandfather laughed aloud, "Your son is smarter than you. At his age, you answered 'Monkey.'"

Anew

It had been ten days since she had asked her employer, and she was resolute not to leave without getting as the festival was on the next day. When she finally got what she had asked for, she rushed home to her eagerly waiting kids. On the morning of the festival, her children bragged about their new dresses to their fellow slum kids, and she silently thanked her employer for donating the old clothes.

Immortal Love

The Angel of Death appeared before the elderly couple to take away the husband. He vehemently rebuked and asked to take his wife instead. The baffled yet loving wife pleaded and persuaded the angel to grant her husband's wish, and he reluctantly took her. The old man then burst  into tears and cried inconsolably, remembering his promise when they fell in love: "I'll never leave you alone!"

Little Surprise

"Mamma, please buy that orange color saree for your birthday," pleaded the little girl. Her mom didn't like it much and tried to convince her, but she was adamant. As the daughter was annoyingly persistent, the  mother reluctantly bought the orange saree. When they were back home, the girl rushed to her room, brought a gift box that she had already bought with her pocket money and wished her mother, "Happy birthday, Mamma!" The mother excitedly opened the box and found inside orange bangles!

Madly in Love

With a jerk, he started running across the busy road. With one hand on the railing, he jumped over the divider. The incoming truck screeched to a halt, missing him by chance of luck. He bent down and scooped her puppy, which was about to be crushed. Spectators called it madness; he called it love!

The Choice

The supervisor summoned the widow, who was a mother of two kids and a daily wage laborer. He persuaded her to compromise with him so that she could give a good standard of living and education to her kids. He also warned her that she wouldn't be able to buy even a morsel of food otherwise. She gave it a thought and nodded. They remained hungry!

Anything for You!

His friends ridiculed him, the neighborhood men smirked at him, and even his parents stopped talking to him. Not faltered, he prepared dinner, fed his baby and video-called his wife. After briefing each other about their days, he asked, "When's your next flight?" "Getting ready," she  replied, looking at her baby with a rueful smile. "Don't worry. I'll take care of our daughter. Fly high, my pilot wife," said he blowing her a kiss - the househusband who sacrificed his career for his wife's dreams!

Bold and Beautiful

Standing sideways in front of the mirror, she admired herself. With perfectly trimmed eyebrow, full lips enhanced by matte lipstick and light makeup, she smiled to herself confidently and started to office. As she turned to pick her handbag up, the mirror reflected the other side of her face, disfigured in an accident!

The Happy Widow

The young widow was playing with her toddler in the park, both laughing heftily. The neighborhood women eyed and bad-mouthed her, saying, "How heartless of her to rejoice within days of her husband's demise!" as she crossed. Back home, she cried aloud at their comments, and the baby started crying seeing her. She quickly wiped her tears and smiled again for her daughter!

My Big Cat

The little girl wrote, "I love lions. They are like big cats with long fluffy hair that I wish to brush. They're quiet, friendly animals and play with humans. I would like to hug it tight and jump on its back for a ride. I can't wait to see the lion again in the circus!"

King's Life

He received VIP treatment wherever he went. Relatives and friends thronged his house, and he gifted them generously from what he got. His wife cooked his favorite meals every day, and his young kids were always by his side. He

felt like he was living a king's life until the day he had to leave back to his work in a distant land with a heavy heart. Having spent all that he had earned, he had to work as a slave for the next three years to live the king's life again in his one-month holiday!

Angel

The white man standing on the pavement was suddenly pushed aside by a plumpy black woman. He, being a racist, detested being touched by the dark-skinned lady. As he was about to yell at her, a car screeched by, nearly missing him, and stopped where he was standing before. Shaken, he looked around for his Guardian Angel, but she was nowhere to be seen. God smiled and said, "Not all angels are fair and beautiful!"

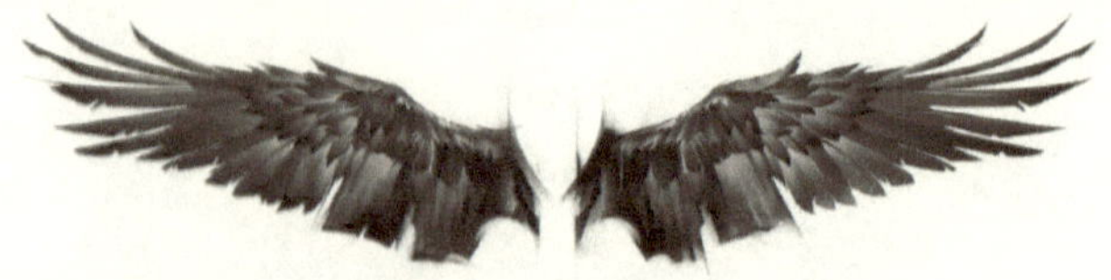

Dreamy Life

He grabbed her hands reassuringly, and they walked along the seashore with waves periodically fondling their feet. Suddenly, he stopped her at the spot where they first met and blindfolded her. She opened her eyes, and he wasn't there. She closed her eyes; he removed the  *blindfold, and she saw a diamond ring. As she exclaimed in joy, he bent on his knees and proposed … in her dreams!*

Body Shaming

The little boy voraciously picked up packets of chips and chocolates in the supermarket. His mom snarled, "If you eat too much junk food, you'll become a butterball like her," pointing fingers at the obese woman taking bread and biscuits nearby. Though hurt, she still smiled gently at the boy and started for her medical appointment with the endocrinologist for hypothyroidism, which caused her abnormal weight gain, giving away the food to the homeless on the way!

Divine Love

On their third wedding anniversary, the couple decided to list down what they wanted to change in each other. After they finished writing, the wife started reading out her list first, which lasted for an hour. Patiently listening, the husband handed over his note and left teary-eyed, which read, "My dear better half, I love you just the way you are!"

Perception of Love

Though the pain was excruciating, he fought the attackers and saved his crush, who was in love with his best friend. After uniting them happily, the hero chose to remain single forever. The father exclaimed that the movie was epic, while his teen son tagged it as bullshit. #generationgap

Annabelle

To prank Samantha, Jennifer bought an Annabelle doll and placed it on Samantha's shelf at midnight and made scary sounds. Jolting up from sleep, Samantha got scared. The following nights, Jennifer kept it inside Samantha's bag and then on the chair facing her. Samantha shivered, screamed and ran out of the room, which made Jennifer laugh out loud. When she heard another voice laughing with her, Jennifer turned only to see the Annabelle doll sitting on her bed. When her eyes widened in fear, it stopped laughing, tilted its head, smirked at her and the door bolted by itself!

Status

To distract herself, she facebooked. Her friends had posted pictures of their husbands in their stories with the captions "Special lunch by my hubby", "Terrace photoshoot with my love" and "Daddy time for kids." She felt her throat tighten and tears trickled down her face. Quickly wiping them away, she posted with pride, "My husband is treating Covid-19 patients for the third week straight!"

Note: This story is dedicated to the doctors and other frontline workers who valiantly fought to protect us during the Covid-19 pandemic.

The Sleeping Beauty

One evening, everyone on the bus laughed at the straphanger who slept standing with her drools dribbling. Her head hitting the handle pole as the bus braked even didn't deter her from sleep. Some recorded her and captioned "The Sleeping Beauty" while others ridiculed her. But what they didn't know was that this hard-working lady wakes up at a time which was still midnight for them!

Poor Life

"You die with your family if you can't repay the loan," the money lender berated the poor man who has been jobless for months now. With those harsh words echoing in his ears, he stared at the rope, knife and pesticides in front of him. Looking at his starving kids and saddened wife, he took them and started to seek job at the nearby coconut farm.

The Creative Child

His classmates mocked his clumsily-stuck cardboard building with hand-drawn windows and surroundings that he brought for his school project day as a skyscraper. Even the visitors hardly stopped by his desk but thronged around those perfectly finished projects that  were either done by the other children's parents or bought ready-made from shops. Discouraged, the child's creativity committed suicide!

Last Day

"I have only a few hours of life left," she realized. Unperturbed, she smiled at a stranger whose face lit up at her beauty. She basked in the sun, danced with the wind, offered what she possessed to visitors and enjoyed everything around her. Living her life to the fullest, the beautiful yet short-lived flower withered away.

Pretense

The wife eagerly served her husband his favorite dishes, anticipating appreciation. He gulped them down, spilling food around, engrossed in his mobile. Without commenting on the taste of his breakfast, he washed his hands over the soiled plate and rushed to the office. There, a colleague  shared her homemade sweets, which he relished eating and praised as a delicacy. He then carefully picked the crumbs and disposed of them. His colleagues wondered, *"How gentle. His wife is very lucky!"*

Red Rose

Bunches of roses were stacked for Valentine's Day. The little girl demanded one from her dad, who was a daily wager. The cost of one rose was Rs. 50, with which his entire family could eat dinner. He dragged the adamantly crying child home; she refused to eat and sobbed to sleep. The following morning, the father patted her hair gently, whispering to open her eyes — she saw a red rose sapling!

Reality

After a heated argument with her husband, she continued reading the novel to ease her mood. *After some time, he came and hugged her from behind. She felt his warm breath on her ears, and he slowly kissed the back of her neck.* Wanting the same thing that she was reading in the book,  she looked at her husband, but he was still angry. Irked, she tossed the book away!

The Philanthropist

On the eve of a charity event where the renowned politician was giving away freebies to the underprivileged, the city was festooned with banners for it. A poor woman carrying her baby came to the laborer setting one such giant banner standing on a scaffold and begged him for money. Looking at their hunger-prone eyes, he gave them a soiled fifty-rupee note, the only money left in his worn-out wallet, and continued tying the banner which hailed the politician "The Philanthropist!"

The Dominant Love

A young woman went to a restaurant with her grandparents. While her grandmother was using the restroom, the waiter arrived at their table. She ordered her breakfast, and the grandfather ordered idly and vada for himself and pongal and coffee  for his wife. "Grandpa, stop being a male chauvinist. You should let grandma order her food", she advised her grandfather, who remained silent. When her grandmother came, she eagerly asked, "Grammy, what do you want to eat?" Her grandmother replied, "Pongal and coffee," looking at her husband, who smiled with love and understanding!

Love Beats

"Papa, grandma says momma died giving birth to me," said the little girl sadly. He scooped his daughter up, placed her on his lap and said, "No, sweety. Your mom is still alive inside me. Want to hear her?" He pressed her ears gently against his chest. Listening to his heartbeat, she exclaimed, "Yes, but I don't understand what momma says," she said, shaking her head innocently. Brushing away his tears, he replied, "You'll understand when you grow up," and hugged her tight. She happily nodded, kissed his chest and said, "Love you, momma!"

Memories

She entered the orphanage hesitantly and saw a boy sitting on the swing all alone. She pitied the little soul and wondered if he had ever felt the touch of love, affectionate kisses, warm hugs and surprise gifts. Her thoughts were interrupted by his question, "You've come  alone. You don't have anyone either?" Clearing her tightening throat, she, who lost her family recently in an accident, neared him and replied, "Yes, but I have their memories." He asked in a mellowing voice, "Will you give me some?" She smiled and pushed his swing, and he exclaimed, "Gee!" in glee, making new memories!

The Mirror

Standing in front of her grandma's antique mirror, she started singing and combing her hair. Seconds later, another voice sang back. Perplexed, she asked, "Who's that?" and it repeated back. Frantically looking around, she noticed the 'Talking Tom' app opened on her mobile. Feeling silly, she left the room, not noticing her image in the mirror staring at her!

Appreciation

Since her son came to work from home almost a year back, she prepared special dishes for him every day and enjoyed watching him eat, even though he didn't appreciate her cooking. That day, she had cooked his favorite biryani and was eagerly awaiting

her son. But he came out enraged after an appraisal discussion with his manager and complained about how his hard work was never recognized. He gobbled up the food and rushed back to work, not noticing the same disappointment on his mother's face once again!

Mansion Pride

He admired the massive mansion he had built, gleaming in the moonbeam. His eyes glinted with pride at his years of hard work, his dream for decades to build one getting its final shape. Mentally calculating the remnant work and content with the progress, entered the thatched hut nearby and slept soundly, the Mason.

Damma

"Ma, open this toy box," "Ma, take me to the park," "Ma, I need new crayons," "Ma, I want to pee," "Ma, I'm hungry," "Ma … Ma … Ma!" the call always echoed in the home. Seeing her husband undisturbed, she thought of a plan and told her son in a mellowing tone,

"Sweetie, hereafter call me 'Daddy,' okay?" hoping her husband would share some responsibilities. The following day onwards, the little boy started calling her "Daddy Ma … Daddy Ma," which soon became "Damma," and the daddy never understood what it meant!

Move On

She jumped in puddles with tribal kids laughing aloud, lovingly stroked the wildflowers alongside the road, relaxedly sat on the lakeshore with legs tucked up and admired the majestic mountain mirrored in the lake. Suddenly, dark clouds moved over. She lifted her chin and smiled as the drizzles spotted her face, wondering if her ex-boyfriend had moved on too.

The Third Door

Standing in front of two doors, the heart was wondering which one to enter. Entering the first one might end up in mockery. But the second will be total backlash, for sure. Contemplating so, started walking away from the restroom doors marked "Men" and "Women" with heart aching more than abdomen, the transgender!

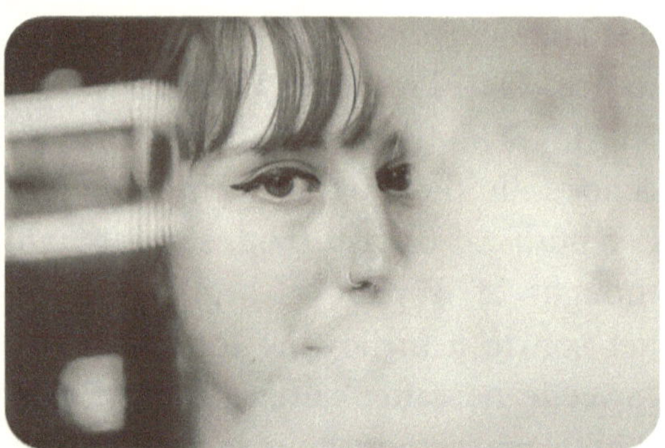

Little Love Stealer

The parents proudly clapped at their one-year-old girl, splashing around the food, trying to eat by herself. Wanting the same love, their five-year-old son also spilled the food around, imitating the baby but was scolded for making a mess. The innocent boy cried, "My parents love only my baby sister. They appreciate her for whatever she does but scold me for everything!"

A Century-Old Love!

On a starry night, the lovers were lying on the lawn admiring the sky. Turning to her side, holding her hands close to his heart and looking into her eyes, he said, "I want to live with you a hundred more years like this," and a shooting star passed by. A hundred years later, the old male and  female tortoises were walking slowly hand in hand on the lawn, and the stars twinkled, winking!

Possessiveness

She called her husband excitedly, "Come home soon, darling! Your favorite biryani is ready. Our boys are already drooling over it." But the husband came home with a pizza, and their sons guzzled it down, ignoring her biryani. The irate wife glared at her husband, who neared her smiling, and said, "Every time you prepare biryani, they eat all of it. Pizzas can be bought, but your biryani is the tastiest and matchless. Can't I be possessive?" Seeing her flush turn to blush, his lips first tasted the smiling hers! 

The Idly Teacher

The stern and inept English teacher was teaching, incorrectly pronouncing the word "idle" as "idly." A smart student in the class got up and corrected him. Infuriated, he punished the student and continued teaching incorrectly for the rest of his career, unaware of being mocked with the nickname "The Idly Teacher."

The Pain

He tried concentrating on the book, but the pain was hurting. Closing it, he went for a walk; he still felt the pain. He began jogging; the pain started to ease. He then did some cardio in the gym; the pain seemed to vanish. The moment he sat to relax, panting, he was overwhelmed by the agonizing pain— the pain of her thoughts!

The Hungry Canine

The ravenous nursing street dog's stomach growled with hunger that she would even eat a human baby. As fate would have it, when  searching for food from a dustbin, she sniffed a newborn baby wrapped in a towel. Snarling her teeth, she pulled the baby out by towel and onto the street and started licking it. Then, she barked aloud, alerted the people around and continued searching for food to feed her puppies!

Beautiful Mother

The kids got frightened. The men gazed disgustingly. The neighbors closed their doors. Walking with gruesome pain, the only thing that worried her was what would be her little daughter's reaction on seeing her face, now scarred because of the acid attack by her drunkard husband. But on seeing her back from the hospital, the daughter ran toward her smiling and hugged her tight.

That's Fate, Mate

The extensive humiliation by his friends on project day challenged him to design a real-time time machine. He went back in time to project day to prevent the haunting humiliation from happening, but a technical glitch in the machine made him live through that incident twice which he had wanted to change!

Profusion

I wanted to pause for a moment and admire nature, but I was pushed from behind.

I wished to listen to the distant koel sing, but I heard murmurs around.
Closing my eyes, I waited on the seashore for the waves to touch and tickle my feet. But suddenly, there were splashes of salt water and sand over me.
#population

Dogs

"You, dog! How dare you enter our area? Let's teach this dog a lesson!" the angry mob thrashed the poor man from another community,

surrounded by passive onlookers who were watching without helping the victim, and some even recorded videos. Accidentally, a stray dog nearby was hit, and it wailed in pain. Hearing its cry, all the dogs from the vicinity bolted to its rescue!

Crazy Daisy

The heavily pregnant woman traveling in public transport was watching a video. She laughed aloud, suddenly jerking her fellow passengers. They soon got irritated and started muttering when she guffawed, watching the same video again and again. Ignoring them, she continued laughing and replaying that particular scene for her baby kicked once again inside!

Selfie Freak

The selfie freak senselessly took selfies in front of an oncoming train, the brink of a hill and even at an accident site and uploaded them to Instagram. Later, his friends teased him about a girl he had posed with in the photos posted. Confused, he viewed his mobile gallery and was shocked to find the girl's selfie with him when he was asleep. Scrolling down, he saw that girl died in an accident where he had clicked a pic earlier, and as he kept staring at the phone, she turned her half-crushed head and growled at him!

Killer

The husband snuck into the room. *The wife pretended to be asleep.* He quickly grabbed the gun. *She felt a lump in her throat.* He started shooting violently. *Flooded tears flowed down the corner of her eyes.* Yet another night, she slept alone with her husband playing PUBG.

Achievement

With his family watching excitedly, the thirteen-year-old pulled the drawer open, took the talcum powder pack, twisted and unlocked the cap, dispensed the powder on his hands and applied it on his face for the first time and smiled. The family cheered aloud for doing it himself and hugged the teen who is autistic!

Untouched

When he came, she prayed, "*Pick me, pick me!*" Her heart skipped a beat when his hands came near, and her joy knew no bounds when he embraced her. When he brought her home, she thought it was love at first sight. But now, she remained a virgin with her cover even untouched…the book unread.

Education

She was furious at her maid for not arriving on time and started doing the dishes. Her teen daughter came to help, but she asked her daughter to go and study. Just then, the maid's ten-year-old daughter turned up with the excuse that her mom was unwell and started cleaning the home, looking desirously at her employer's daughter who was studying aloud, "The right to education is one of the fundamental rights in the Indian Constitution…"

Burned

On a hot summer evening, when the wind seemed to be on strike and the leaves barely moving, the wife was preparing dinner in the kitchen with sweat beads traversing the length of her body. At her husband's call, she prepared roti in a hurry and accidentally burned her finger. Ignoring it, she served dinner to her husband, who spat out his first mouthful, complaining of its poor taste. For the first time, she realized her finger pain!

The Rainbow

After rainfall, she prayed to God for a rainbow. She ran and peeped through the small window but was saddened to see none. And the entire season, she kept praying for a rainbow, looking out the window every day in vain. Feeling dejected, she finally gave up. Yet, God kept the rainbow shining—only had she stepped outside the house to see it!

The Dream

She had the same dream once again: She was in a beautiful garden with colorful flowers, but when she touched one, it withered away. Colleagues suggested that she consult a pranic healer; friends advised her to get psychiatrist counseling; and her parents insisted she see a sorcerer, but she visited a horticulturist. Soon, the dream garden was grown, and now, when she touched the flowers, they didn't wither away!

Spoiled Generation

"Papa, please take him to the park. He's watching YouTube all day," the screen-addicted kid's mom requested her father. In the park, the grandfather pushed his grandson's swing as he checked Facebook on his phone. He excitedly played on the slide and noticed that his grandpa was reading the online news, occasionally smiling at him. The grandson was waiting for his grandpa to balance the seesaw but noticed that he was watching WhatsApp videos one after the next. The boy rushed back home and continued watching rhymes!

Modern Cinderella

When Cinderella wept that her stepsisters left for the prince's ball, disregarding her, her godmother appeared and magically transformed the pumpkin into a Porsche and a lizard into a driver and made her as beautiful as a doll. She also gifted her a smartphone but warned that she should be home by midnight or else the spell would be broken. At the ball, the prince, mesmerized by her beauty, chatted and danced only with Cinderella. When the clock struck 12, Cinderella rushed back, leaving behind her smartphone in a hurry. The desperate prince searched every house, holding Cinderalla's phone in front of every girl to unlock the phone with face recognition, but in vain. Finally, when Cinderella appeared in her own self, the prince held the phone to her face, and it unlocked. When the prince jumped in ecstasy, Cinderella said politely, "If my phone could recognize me without makeup, but you couldn't, you don't deserve me."

www.ingramcontent.com/pod-product-compliance
Lightning Source LLC
Chambersburg PA
CBHW021525160726
47989CB00019B/1876